THE WARRIOR'S PROMISE

I promise to be a good student,

to feed my mind,

to strengthen my body,

to have truth in my heart,

to be kind and always do my best.

This story is dedicated to all the little
monkeys in my own school whose struggles
and successes inspire us every day.—M.C.S.

For my Mum, for all the love, support and
constant babysitting.—S.B.

OXFORD
UNIVERSITY PRESS

Great Clarendon Street, Oxford OX2 6DP
Oxford University Press is a department of the University of Oxford.
It furthers the University's objective of excellence in research, scholarship,
and education by publishing worldwide. Oxford is a registered trade mark
of Oxford University Press in the UK and in certain other countries

Text copyright © Oxford University Press 2019
Illustrations copyright © Steve Brown 2019
Author photo © Joe Worby

British Library Cataloguing in Publication Data

Data available

ISBN 9780192771711

1 3 5 7 9 10 8 6 4 2

Printed in India

Paper used in the production of this book is a natural,
recyclable product made from wood grown in sustainable forests.
The manufacturing process conforms to the environmental
regulations of the country of origin.

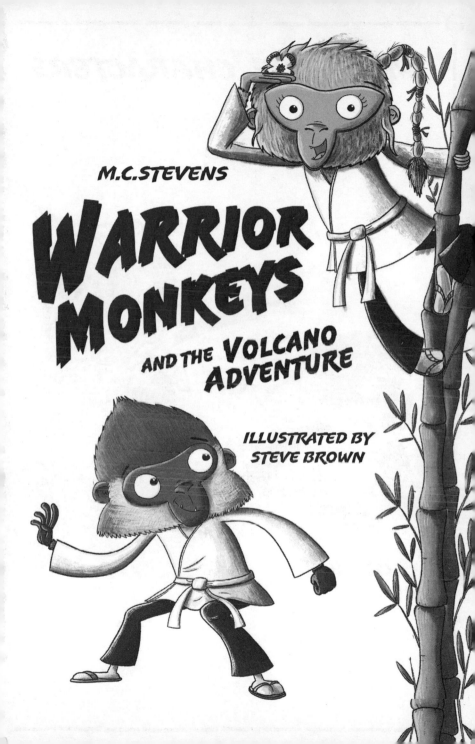

M.C.STEVENS

WARRIOR MONKEYS

AND THE VOLCANO ADVENTURE

ILLUSTRATED BY
STEVE BROWN

MEET THE CHARACTERS

SUKI

BEKKO

FARA

CHAN

SENSEI RIKA

JIRUGI

TENGU

PROLOGUE

Tied up and under guard, Jirugi still looked dangerous. He was large even for a mandrill: the strongest of the monkeys. His face was dirty after the long fight but his eyes glowed with rage as Master Chan rose to give the Kuro council's decision.

'Jirugi, the Warrior Monkeys have no choice. You have betrayed the values of kindness and justice that make our law. You have continued to use your strength

to abuse others and shown no remorse for your actions. We banish you from the Shanti Islands with immediate effect. Do you have anything to say?'

Jirugi spat on the floor, an act of disrespect that caused several of the Kuro to wince. There was an almost imperceptible rattle of wooden armour as the guard bears quivered with anger. Their simple loyalty to the warrior code was absolute: an insult to the Kuro was an insult to all the Warrior Monkeys and to all creatures who shared the Shanti Islands. Their prisoner had plenty more to add.

'I don't care about your laws of weakness and wishy-washy nonsense,

Chan! If you think the islands can be kept safe with good deeds and bravery then you're even more stupid than I thought. Power is for the strong, and it needs to be used by the strongest; for the good of everyone!'

Master Chan sighed, sorrowfully shaking his head at his former student. 'I don't regret giving you so many chances to find a better path, Jirugi. But I do regret the pain you have caused us all, and it now has to stop. We will take you over the sea to Gimandesh and you can make a new start. You can never return here. Is that clear?'

'Am I supposed to be grateful for this new start? Ridiculous! If you really wanted to protect your precious islands you would kill me, but you don't have the guts. Let's get this over with. I've had enough of your pathetic teaching. I've learned nothing from you.'

Chan swept back his magnificent hair and his calm, strong face seemed etched with wisdom, sadness, and resolution.

'Learned nothing . . . well, that much seems to be true. Guards, take him away.'

SIX YEARS LATER

CHAPTER ONE

The sound of the castle's bell carried south on the wind as it clanged the summons to morning training. Young Warrior Monkeys ran to prepare themselves: the hall must be swept; uniforms must be tidied; hair tied back; and all should be kneeling in neat rows to await the beginning of the lesson. Neat and tidy, organized and disciplined. This was the way of the warrior.

Two monkeys had not responded to the bell. One of these was Suki, ignoring the distant noise as she balanced lightly on a maple branch. She was looking at the stony ledge high above and wondering if she could jump that far. The other was her friend, Bekko, who was pleading with her to come down.

'Suki!' he begged. 'Please hurry! We're going to be late for class again. Sensei will be furious!'

'Just a few more seconds. I'm soooo close.'

Even for a warrior monkey, Suki had super agility. Her jumping and climbing skills were known for getting her out of tricky situations. Right now, though,

Bekko knew his friend was leaping into trouble. She had never succeeded in raiding the squirrels' nut store high up on the slippery rock face. He knew it wasn't even that she wanted the nuts for herself. It was all about the challenge!

The bell rang again and Bekko looked desperately up the mountain, watching the Warrior Monkey students running through the big castle gates. Above him, Suki crouched low then exploded suddenly into her jump. She was a flying crescent in the air, stretching wildly for the ledge . . . and missing again. Bump, scrape, bash, splat. Down she came and the squirrels all raced out on the ledge to laugh at her, taunting her with the

nuts she tried so hard to steal. She took
a deep breath and rubbed her bruised
legs. Nothing broken. But . . . the bell
had stopped. Looking up the mountain
towards the castle they could see the
gates had closed. This time they would be
in deep trouble, and Bekko struggled not
to cry. He hated being late, and dreaded
the punishment they would get. He sank

to the ground despairingly, head in his hands.

'Suki! Now look what's happened! Why didn't you just come when I asked you?'

Suki was immediately very sorry. She didn't mind too much about being punished, but she did mind about upsetting her friend.

'Bekko, I'm so sorry. This is all my fault.'

'Well maybe next time you will listen to me!' he said, sadly. He knew his adventurous friend had a lot to learn about being a true warrior.

'Come on then,' she said, pulling him up by the elbow. 'We might get back before they finish warming up if we hurry.' She set off towards the castle at a brisk jog, not noticing that Bekko had stayed rooted to the spot.

'Hey! Suki! Come back!' he shouted, waving his arms. She stopped, surprised, and scampered back quickly, wondering what could distract Bekko from getting back immediately.

'Look at the volcano!' he exclaimed, pointing through the rocky forest to where the twin peaks of Mount Niru and Mount Leng marked the horizon. Mount Leng was a jagged mountain; its trees and cliffs were exciting to explore. Streams sliced their way down towards the ocean and offered great opportunities

for leaping and swimming. Mount Niru was different, however. It was a dormant volcano and the stink of sulphur gas escaping from it was already enough to put off anyone keen to visit. It was covered in low, prickly bushes that were no fun for the monkeys, who enjoyed high trees. Usually it only attracted Bekko's interest when he wanted to see the playful meerkats who lived on its slopes. Now, however, he was staring at a low cloud that hung over the crater.

'Suki! That cloud is all wrong!'

Suki couldn't see anything peculiar about the cloud. Surely it was just a cloud?

'What do you mean, Bekko?' she

asked, impatiently. 'There's lots of clouds around today!'

'Not like that!' He was shaking his head and looking very concerned. 'It's the wrong shape. It's the wrong height. It's the wrong colour! I think it's an ash cloud.'

Suki couldn't believe that Bekko was more interested in the clouds than in getting back to the castle.

'Seriously, Bekko! I don't care what kind of cloud it is! Can we go? You were the one upset about being late and now you're fussing about the shape of a cloud! Hurry up!'

Bekko really wanted to explain to Suki why the cloud was important, but he

could see that she wasn't listening. In
fact, she had already set off again up the
path towards the castle. He shrugged
and ran after her. As they knocked on
the castle gates, he looked back again.
Maybe if he could explain to Sensei Rika
she would understand. But the cloud had
gone. As the big wooden gate creaked
open, he tried to put the worry out of

his head. This wasn't too difficult with Kuma, the giant guard bear, glaring at them and shaking his shaggy head crossly.

'What were you thinking? You know lateness is unacceptable at Senshi Castle. We expect better of you! Get to class straight away. You'd better hope that Sensei Rika is in a forgiving mood!'

'Yes, Kuma! Sorry, Kuma! Thank you, Kuma!' They scurried past him apologetically and raced to class as if their tails were on fire.

Sensei Rika raised an eyebrow in their direction as they slipped through the door of the training hall. They knelt down and waited. Silently. Respectfully. Patiently.

'Perhaps you would like to join us?' When Sensei finally invited them into the line, they performed their two ceremonial bows quickly and carefully and took their places. They had missed most of the warm up and the class was already on basic punching. Bekko launched into his front punches with total focus. Each student took it in turn to count aloud for ten punches while Sensei walked up and down the lines checking technique and effort. When it was Bekko's turn to count, he shouted as loudly as he could. He tried so hard that his voice cracked on number nine; he blushed deeply and stuttered on ten. Could this day get any worse? He could hear a stifled giggle behind him and a whisper:

'N-n-nice counting, B-B-Bekko!'

He didn't know who it was, and didn't dare look. He was sadly used to the older monkeys teasing him. It could have been any of them. Nita, who enjoyed it when others were in trouble. Yash, who had a nasty habit of mimicking Bekko to make the others laugh. Or Kang. Kang loved to try to wind Bekko up until he lost control and exploded with his voice or his fists.

Suki saw Bekko grit his teeth and look down at the floor. She had not heard what had happened but she knew the signs.

'Ignore them!' she growled, under cover of the counting. Sensei was at the back of the class. The last thing they both needed was more trouble today, but she hated seeing Bekko upset.

The class moved on to blocking work. The rows of students turned to face each other; Suki found herself opposite Kang as Sensei Rika called out combinations.

'Face punch, rising block!'

'Body punch, outer block!'

Kang's punches were rapid and strong; it took all Suki's concentration to apply the correct blocks to stop herself being hit. Around her the noises of breathing intensified as the class picked up an energetic, absorbing rhythm. The

exercises allowed her to put aside her worries about Bekko and the punishment they might receive until finally the drills came to an end. They sat to stretch and listen while Sensei spoke. She used the end of each session to teach her pupils the ideas and rules of their training. It was not enough to fight well. They needed to develop the heart and mind of a warrior to show they could truly earn the right to be called Warrior Monkeys.

Bekko squirmed on his mat, already knowing what today's lesson would be.

'What is the first rule of the warrior?' asked Sensei Rika.

'Courtesy!' they all chanted back.

'And courtesy means?'

'Always treat others as you would like to be treated!'

'So, this includes always being on time. Does it not, Suki?'

'Yes, Sensei.' Suki nodded then looked down at her toes. She was surprised to see quite how battered they were from falling onto the rocks earlier.

'Bekko. What is the rule about punctuality?' Sensei glared at him. He coughed, and drew his shoulders back. Then he spoke clearly and firmly.

'That to be early is to be on time. To be on time is to be late. To be late . . . is unforgiveable, Sensei.'

'Indeed.'

CHAPTER TWO

Sensei Rika was swift to set their punishments.

'Obviously I cannot let this go with just a warning. It would not help you if I were to simply shake a finger and then send you off to play. You should be thankful for the opportunity this gives you to think about why this is important, and try harder next time. While the other students have their trip to the other

islands today, you will go and help in the kitchen and the garden.'

Bekko was devastated to miss the boat trip. They would have been visiting the library on the island of Silla and it was his favourite place in the world. His face was a picture of misery and his head dropped. But he did quite like helping in the garden . . . maybe it wasn't going to be a total disaster? Ah. No. It was the worst.

'Bekko!'

'Yes, Sensei?'

'Report to the kitchen immediately.'

'Yes, Sensei!' His voice was as respectful as ever, though his feet dragged as he set off. Now Suki didn't know which to feel worse about—causing Bekko's punishment, or having to cope with her own, which was . . .

'Gardening for you, Suki. I'm sure some time spent with Master Chan will help your focus.'

Uh oh. This was going to be torture. She wanted to argue with Sensei: offer to clean the training hall; run some errands; do a thousand press-ups; anything!

'Please no, Sensei! I really am sorry.
I won't do it again! Let me help Fara
instead of Bekko! None of this was his
fault!'

'Bekko is responsible for being on time
by himself. He doesn't have to be late to
keep you company, Suki. That's not your
business. It is my business to help you to
learn to do better. And I choose to send
you to Chan. Off you go.'

Suki wanted so much to rebel against
Sensei's instructions even though she
knew that arguing would make it worse.
It would have been such a relief to shout
'NO!' and just run off into the woods.
For a second, she nearly chose to do
that, then she thought about Kuma and

how upset and angry he would be. And
he would be right. She needed to face
her punishment. 'Get up, Suki. Get on
with it, Suki,' she told herself firmly.
She bowed speedily to Sensei Rika and
zoomed away to get it over with.

While Suki was rushing to the serene
gardens, Bekko had dragged himself to
the hectic castle kitchen. He hovered at
the kitchen door a moment, taking in the
scene before him.

Fara, the short, plump kitchen
dragon, stood stir-frying vegetables in
a huge pan. She wore an apron that was
covered in splashes and stains. As she
tossed the vegetables high in the air she

hummed tunelessly, every now and then breaking out into a few lines of song. The happy words seemed to be about flying through the mountains, flaming the forests beneath. Every time she sang 'Burn! Destroy!' she would stamp her feet merrily and throw the pea pods with extra energy. Bekko edged in meekly to wait until she finished.

Whenever Bekko had to take his turn in the kitchen, he would be flustered and often slightly fearful. You could never tell if Fara was about to flamegrill the floor with a sneeze, or knock over a stack of plates with her wayward tail as she dashed up and down the stoves.

'Ah, Bekko!' she huffed cheerfully, parking her frying pan to one side and reaching for one of her long skewers. 'Help me with these banana fritters, will you?' Bekko sighed, knowing that to hold the skewer for fritters was likely to end in some singed fingers. Fara's aim with her flame was not great. But he took the skewer as asked, and in fact was only mildly toasted.

'So, what were you thinking, Bekko, making yourself late for class?' she said. It was typical of Fara to jump straight to the point.

'Ah . . .' began Bekko.

'Your training is more important than waiting around for Suki.' It was also typical of her not to wait for an answer. She swept on, her words scorching Bekko just like her flames had grilled the fritters. 'Warrior Monkeys have to stand up for themselves! You can't keep letting yourself follow Suki into mischief.' Fara was shaking her wooden spatula at him to emphasize her words.

'I care about Suki and she doesn't mean to get me in trouble. I don't want her to think I'm bossing her around. Maybe she would be angry with me if I nagged her all the time.' Bekko's fear of losing Suki as a friend was clear in his voice.

'You don't have to nag her all the time!' Fara snapped firmly. 'If it is important to you then Suki will respect what you say. If not, then is she really the friend you deserve?'

'I s-s-s-uppose so.' Bekko felt uncomfortable at the idea of standing up for himself to Suki. But he could also see that Fara was right, because Suki didn't mean to get him in trouble. She just didn't think the same way that he did.

'Well, then it's time to change things. Not all at once. One good decision at a time. How do you eat an elephant?'

Bekko laughed. 'I don't eat elephants! But yes, I know. One bite at a time, not all at once.'

The little dragon smiled at him. 'Correct! It's time to think about the future, Bekko. With your discipline, your knowledge, your kindness, you should be training for leadership. So should your scruffy little friend, despite everything!'

Bekko had heard this from Fara before but he always thought she was just trying to encourage him. This time, though, she seemed fiercely serious.

'You can't understand how important it is for these islands to have good leaders. You know the stories about Jirugi?'

Bekko nodded. Jirugi was the strong monkey who had tried to take over the Shanti Islands. This was a bitter memory for the older islanders and they often used Jirugi as a warning for the young warriors.

'If the islands are to be safe from Jirugi, or monkeys like him, we need brave, kind leaders. He's gone, but who knows when he'll come back? And he'd have no hesitation to use bad power to get what he wants.'

Bekko felt alarmed. This was not the sort of thing that Sensei Rika was teaching them in her classes. Bad power?

'What do you mean, bad power? Do you mean magic?' he asked.

'Magic isn't bad. It depends who is using it!' explained Fara. 'Warrior Monkeys share with magical creatures like me, but we all agree to be kind and fair. No one person holds all the power. I bet Jirugi wouldn't hesitate to use magical creatures to get what he wants. We all need to be ready. Be brave, be kind, do your best, Bekko. That's how we train. But you know this in your heart. Now, let's chop this squid, shall we? One squid at a time!' she said cheerily.

Bekko shuddered. He had particular trouble with strong smells or unusual textures. Fara always seemed to have fish on the menu. Stinky, slimy fish. It felt disgusting. It smelt disgusting. How he hated fish!

'One squid at a time,' Bekko repeated
sadly, eyeing up
the mountain
of squid on the
table. It did seem
overwhelming. He
wondered briefly
if he would rather
eat an elephant,
and the silliness of
the thought made
him smile a little.
Sighing, he took a
small squid from
the pile and started to chop.

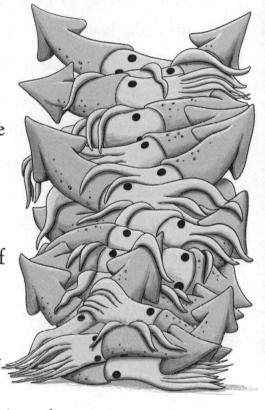

Suki was having a very different afternoon, starting with a hunt for Chan.

After a lengthy period of running round the lawns and paths, she spotted him. He was sitting in the water garden where the statues of ancient Warrior Monkeys faced the waterfalls tumbling on smooth stones beneath. Although he sat as still as the statues, she could see his long hair moving in the breeze as he gazed at the rocks.

Chan did not seem to notice her as she skidded to a halt then clattered across the path towards him. She stood awkwardly, waiting for him to look up.

Chan hadn't always been the castle's gardener. In the past he had been

Guardian of Senshi, but he had found it hard to recover after Jirugi's rebellion because Jirugi had been one of his best students. He could have moved to Silla where the gardens were beautiful and the older monkeys studied and trained together. But he liked to be close by to support and advise Sensei Rika.

He believed that growing young warriors was like building a beautiful garden; it took time, patience, and skill. Under his management, Senshi Castle now had a Zen garden with wonderful gravel swirls and shapes. It also had a water garden with intricate springs and channels flowing over coloured pebbles and rocks. And the flower garden, full of

spectacular, clever bursts of colour at all times of year. He was often hard to find; the grounds were huge and he liked to tend every part personally.

'Uh. Ahem. Sir. Excuse me . . .' she ventured eventually.

'Yes, Suki?' came the unhurried response.

'Sensei sent me to help you. I was late again. So I had to come. I can dig. Would you like me to dig? I can carry rocks. Shall I carry rocks? What about the tools? Shall I clean them?'

He sighed. 'Sit with me, Suki. I am watching the stones grow.' Suki's hopeful face dropped. Meditation. Now she had plenty of time to think about the

consequences of being late. Her head
was buzzing with irritation and regret;
her body was struggling with fidgets and
discomfort. She tried hard just to focus
on the stone and the waterfall, to breathe
and to empty her mind. Her brain was
like a racetrack: worry about Bekko kept
whizzing about . . . shame at being late
chased the worry, and then got overtaken
by anger about the students who had
teased Bekko. 'Be calm,' she nagged
herself. 'Calm. Now. Quickly, do it now!
BE CALM!'

'Don't fight with your thoughts, Suki.'
Chan's deep voice was soothing, rather
like the flow of the water. 'Accept the
distractions,' he continued. 'Notice them.

Move them gently to the side to allow yourself to find a clear space. Breathe . . .'

Suki sneaked a look at him out of the corner of her eye. He seemed to glow with wisdom. And he was so still. Determined to try her hardest, Suki gazed at the stones in the water. She wanted to rush into being as still as Chan. She thought about being energetic with stillness and nearly made herself laugh. She pushed away the silly thoughts and tried to breathe deeply. But even when she thought she was sitting still, she seemed to be quivering. Did she imagine it, or was the water also vibrating? Yes! There was definitely a wobble in the water! But then it stopped. She sat, confused. She flickered another sideways

look at Master Chan, who remained
focused on the stones, yet she thought
she detected a slight frown on his face.

'Sir? What was that?' she asked,
timidly.

Chan turned to her, and motioned for
her to remain quiet. He laid his ear to the
ground and listened for a while. Rapid

questions bounced into Suki's mind; she squashed them with an effort and waited respectfully until Chan sat up.

'Well, Suki,' he said thoughtfully, 'I think that was perhaps a small earthquake.'

'An earthquake! Is it dangerous?' Suki asked, alarmed.

'I'm sure it is nothing to worry about. It was very small. We would probably not even have noticed it if we had not been so quiet and still.' Chan's words were reassuring.

'Come, Suki! Let us resume our work.'

Suki sighed, and turned her attention back to the stones. 'Right, you stones,' she thought fiercely. 'Watch out! I'm going to MAKE you grow now.'

It was going to be a long afternoon.

When Suki finally left the garden, she
found Bekko waiting for her in the main
courtyard. She was relieved to share her
frustration with him and her description
of the afternoon made him laugh.

'Stones growing! Stones don't grow,
Bekko. Why does he make me look for
things that aren't there?' she exclaimed.

'Because it helps you to focus, and
to calm your mind, Suki. Warrior
Monkeys must always be able to block
out distractions. It really helps me with
the things I find difficult,' said Bekko,
looking serious.

'Such as?' asked Suki.

'Well, take Kang,' continued Bekko, 'he's always saying things to wind me up. And it used to work. I'd lash out and I'd be the one who would get into trouble. Now I pretend his voice is just water and I am the stone.'

'I know,' sighed Suki. 'You're my friend and I'd always stand up for you, even fight for you . . . but you manage very well on your own these days!' She gave Bekko a hug. 'And I know that Sensei sends me to Chan to help me to make better decisions. If I found it easy, she wouldn't send me. I will try harder. Anyway, how was Fara?'

'Oh, it was soooooo gross, Suki.'

Bekko made a face like he was going to vomit. 'The worst. She made me chop the squid. It was slimy and stinky. I'm sure my hands are still squiddy now, even though I've washed them about a hundred times! And she was really scaring me with her warnings about Jirugi. I was already worried about the weird clouds on the volcano, and now she's got me imagining Jirugi attacking us with an army of magical creatures at any second!'

'Oh, she's always full of nonsense about Jirugi!' Suki said cheerfully. 'I think she's just being dramatic. But something weird happened when I was in the garden. Did you feel an earthquake?'

'An earthquake?' Bekko's eyes nearly popped out of his head. 'No!'

'Well,' Suki said, 'I don't think it was a dangerous one. I just felt the ground vibrating for a few seconds. Chan felt it too, so I know I didn't imagine it. I guess you wouldn't notice with all the noise in the kitchen.'

'What if it was Mount Niru?' Bekko said, with excitement. 'If the ground is rumbling and there is cloud over the crater, then it's possible the volcano will erupt!'

'Why are you excited?' Suki couldn't understand how Bekko might be pleased about this.

He smiled back at her. 'Don't worry

Suki, I'm not crazy. Mount Niru has never erupted over Senshi Island. The eruptions are small, and the lava and ash blow south with the wind. It would be amazing to see though. It only erupts once every fifty years, I think.'

Suki was often impressed and fascinated by the things Bekko knew.

'Wow,' she said. 'I guess it would be pretty cool to see that.'

'It might be nothing,' Bekko added, with a shrug. 'Sometimes a few rumbles turn into an eruption and sometimes they just stop happening. I expect it was just something like that; as far as I remember there's no eruption due for years. I'd really love to go and have a look though.

Wouldn't you?'

'Ooooh, yes, let's!' Suki said enthusiastically. 'When? We can't go now; we'd be late back for dinner. And that's the last thing we need today!'

'What about if we just go tomorrow after lunch?' Bekko suggested. 'We normally go out then anyway, so no one will notice. I think the best plan would be to go up to the top of Mount Leng. There's a perfect view of the volcano from there, without getting too close.'

'Do you think we should tell Kuma where we are going?' Suki asked.

'Actually, I don't think we should, Suki,' he replied, thoughtfully. 'I truly don't think it is dangerous, but Kuma

might not want us to go near Mount Niru
if there could be an eruption. And it's
probably nothing anyway. No one else
seems to have noticed anything. Let's not
worry him for no good reason.'

'Right.' Suki agreed. 'Tomorrow
afternoon, then. It will be fun! And now,
what about a swim before dinner?'

Together they ran down to the beautiful cove beneath the castle, leaping from trees to rocks then launching themselves into the water with a big splash. Bekko was so excited about tomorrow; even knowing there was squid for dinner didn't spoil his mood.

CHAPTER THREE

Early next morning Suki sat in the
gatehouse, trying not to fidget while
Kuma plaited her unruly hair. No
matter how carefully he tidied it with
his dextrous claws, she always ended up
looking like a porcupine by lunchtime. Yet
he persisted with this daily routine and
they would exchange news and thoughts
as he tutted comfortably, combing out
twigs and tangles. Suki always felt that she

could trust Kuma; she liked to chatter to him while he baked or carved his wooden figures. The gentle guard was very fond of his lively companion and did his best to steer her to being more organized and disciplined.

She winced as he pulled her plaits tightly and pinned them back behind her ears.

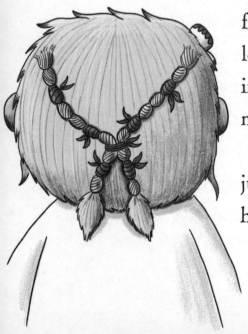

'There,' he said, fondly. 'Now you look like a warrior instead of a kitchen mop.'

She laughed and jumped down from her chair happily.

Unfortunately,
she knocked into
Kuma's work table
as she did so, and
some wooden figures
and cards fell to the
floor.

Ikuchi
Ancient sea serpent.
Oozes stinking oil
which swamps boats.
Rating: 2/5
Mildly mean.

Joroguma
Goblin Spider. Can transform
into any shape in the light.
Reverts to spider-form in
darkness. Tricks its prey and
catches it with its deadly
web. Rating: 4/5
Troublemaker

'Oh! Sorry,
Kuma!' she squealed,
dashing to pick them up again.

'Don't worry, nothing broken!' Kuma
was very used to monkeys bouncing
around his rooms. He helped to pick up
some of the cards.

'This is Bekko's writing, isn't it?' Suki
asked, holding up a handful of cards.

'Yes, we're working on this together.

He's making the descriptions and I'm doing the models.' Kuma sat down and began to sort the cards into neat piles.

'Mystical creatures!' she said. 'What is this one?' She held a snake-like object in her hands. 'Some kind of dragon? But no wings . . .'

'That's an Ikuchi. Here, it goes with the "sea" pile.' He took it from her and placed it carefully with its matching card.

'Ikuchi' she read, picking up the card. 'Ancient sea serpent. Oozes stinking oil which swamps boats. Rating: 2/5: Mildly mean.' Bekko had underlined the 'stinking' part which made Suki laugh as she imagined him wrinkling his nose. Carefully replacing the card she took one

at random from another pile. It was a
horrible-looking spider.

'Jorogumo. Goblin Spider. Can
transform into any shape in the light.
Reverts to spider-form in darkness.
Tricks its prey and catches it with its
deadly web. Rating: 4/5: Troublemaker.'

'I haven't carved that one yet.' Kuma
told her. 'I've been working on the "air"
creatures before the "land" ones. Here,
check out this one I finished yesterday.'

He handed her a carving of a bird
with a nasty sharp beak. It was holding
a long stick and . . . was that a fan? She
shivered. There were no birds anywhere
on the Shanti Islands, and all the Warrior
Monkeys considered them to be evil

spies. This one looked horrible.

'Tengu. Bird demon. Uses fan to control winds and staff to hypnotize weak animals. Bossy and arrogant. Rating: 5/5: Lethal!' she read on Bekko's card. 'Ugh! Show me something nicer, please!'

Tengu.
Bird demon.
Uses fan to control winds and staff to hypnotize weak animals. Bossy and arrogant.
Rating: 5/5
Lethal

'How about this one?' He handed her a little hedgehog, beautifully carved, with its fine prickles.

'Wow, I love it! It doesn't look very mystical though?' She turned it upside down, wondering if she was missing something.

'It's mostly only annoying. Flying hedgehog. We did have some over in Jindo a few years ago, I heard, but I don't know if it was really true. They're not dangerous anyway.' Gently, Kuma took the carving from her and placed it with the cards.

'Hadn't you better find Bekko and scoot along to class? Today would be a very good day to be early for training,

Suki-su!'

He gave her a hug and a slice of banana bread, and she went to find her friend.

First she went to his room. She took a moment to admire the neat lines of stones he had made around the floor. Bekko loved to put things in order, and would collect smooth stones and pebbles wherever they went. When he wanted time to himself he would sit in his room and organize the stones. However, although there were plenty of stones and books, there was no Bekko. He wasn't in the training hall, or in the kitchen. She jogged through the grounds, scanning. Then she spotted him with Chan, quietly cleaning the tools in the kitchen garden.

She stopped a moment to watch before going in. There was no conversation needed between them as they worked calmly and thoroughly, each noticing the other when he needed a cloth or another tool to polish or sharpen. Bekko did not pester Chan with questions, or chatter about his thoughts. He did not fidget when waiting. They worked together like silent music, if such a thing could be real. Suki was impressed. Respectfully, she waited for them to finish instead of rushing in to join them. When Bekko and Chan had put everything away they bowed to each other. Then Chan nodded to Suki.

'Good morning, young Suki.'

'Good morning, sir. I hope you are well.'

'Thank you, Suki, I am indeed. I return your friend to you. And there is the bell for morning class! Off you go! I know you wouldn't want to be late . . .'

She blushed and thanked him. Wishing Chan a good day, they scurried to the training hall to begin preparations for class.

Sensei Rika was working on training their awareness, and Bekko was finding it tough. One monkey stood in the middle of the hall defending the cloth tail tucked into the back of his or her belt. Blindfolded, the challenge was all about listening and moving fast without losing balance as the other monkeys crept in to take turns to try and steal the prize tail.

'Haha, Bekko! Got you! You'll have to be smarter than that to beat me!' Kang dangled a cloth tail in front of Bekko, cackling triumphantly. Bekko had removed his blindfold and he then bowed to Kang.

'Good skills, Kang.' he said respectfully. 'Thank you for the game.'

Sensei nodded to Bekko. She noticed

that he had managed to keep his cool. Although it was clear that his disappointment was strong, the pride of the warrior was stronger. Perhaps he was ready to be challenged a little more.

'Keep the blindfold, Bekko,' she said. 'Let's work on your focus a little.' Kang was especially good at tricking his way to winning the game by making noise on one side then silently sneaking to snatch the tail from the other side. He was a lot bigger than Suki and Bekko, and had recently been graded to cadet level; he was very proud of his short stick and red belt. Although he always made sure to be respectful and controlled when Sensei Rika was watching, it was no surprise

that Kang would swagger and tease the juniors when he thought no one was watching. With their white belts, and no weapons, he clearly thought they would be jealous and impressed by him. Suki secretly thought Sensei knew that Kang was sometimes a bully. She watched with interest as Bekko replaced the blindfold and the game began again.

The class spread out again and sat down in a circle. Bekko stood in the middle with his arms outstretched.

'Without your eyes, you have to work harder with your other senses. Think about what you can hear, what you can feel, what you can smell . . . tell me what you're thinking.' Sensei stood at the edge of the circle, watching Bekko.

'I feel the blindfold is scratchy and uncomfortable,' he said truthfully.

'OK. Let's assume that this will not help you, so you place that feeling into a box for later and find the things that matter,' Sensei advised. Like ignoring the slimy squid, Bekko thought to himself.

'What else can you feel?' she asked him.

'I feel the ground under my feet,' he replied, cautiously, wondering if that sounded stupid.

'Excellent! That's good. What does it feel like?'

'Well, here in the training hall the floor is always clean and smooth—it feels the same everywhere, right?' Bekko tapped his feet around him, showing confidence in his balance.

'Yes.' Sensei Rika nodded to agree. 'So that means . . . ?'

'Erm, I guess it means I can move without tripping?'

'Sure. It's a pretty safe surface. Useful to know, but something else you can set aside for now. What do you hear?'

Bekko tilted his head, considering. 'I hear Fara singing in the kitchen. I hear Kuma stacking the firewood. I hear Ko whispering to Nita.' The littlest Warrior Monkey stopped whispering and looked embarrassed.

'Very good! And finally, what do you

smell?'

Bekko smiled. Smell was always easy for him.

'I smell the flowers through the window,' he said. 'I smell Nita's hair oil. And I can smell Yash's sweat too.' Yash was Kang's best friend—a big monkey who wasn't that keen on regular washing. He scowled but Kang laughed. 'He's not wrong, Yash, you do stink today!'

Sensei shot them a look, and they both immediately sat quietly. She turned back to Bekko.

'So you've got plenty of information even without seeing the room. To succeed you need to decide what is important. Let's try again with the tail.'

Student after student approached Bekko. But now his confidence grew as he won the game repeatedly. By filtering out the 'safe' noises and smells, he could tune in to the approaching tiptoes or breathing of the various monkeys sent to try and trick him. When the game ended they all congratulated Bekko on

his improvement. Even Kang clapped him on the shoulder with a gruff 'Not bad!' which both Suki and Sensei Rika privately noted with satisfaction.

'Line up!' Sensei called them to bow out and they all snapped smartly into line, ready to tidy up for lunch.

CHAPTER FOUR

That afternoon, Bekko and Suki packed
plenty of nuts and snacks ready for
their trek to Mount Leng. They loved to
explore Senshi Island's hills and forests.
Sometimes they went to the coast with
its rocky beaches, sometimes to the
valleys full of streams. Today they felt
they had a mission, though, and lost no
time heading straight to the south where
the sky was dominated by the two big
mountains. They stood at the foot of

Mount Leng with its tall trees and high peak.

'I'll race you to the top!' Suki suggested, turning to Bekko.

Although Bekko was not as agile as Suki, he could still challenge her when they raced together. Suki always took super-ambitious jumps, which were spectacular when successful but she fell frequently. Bekko preferred to take smaller leaps. Sometimes this meant they were neck-and-neck, as Suki was constantly having to pick herself up and climb back up to the green canopy of branches.

'Sure. That silver fir tree on the right? Good finish line?' Bekko pointed to a

beautiful tree at the peak, which offered a great view of the volcano opposite.

'Ready?' Suki was itching to get going, hopping from foot to foot. Bekko took a moment to breathe and decide which tree to go for first.

'Yup.' He and Suki bumped fists and counted down together:

'Ready. Set. Go!'

Suki got a great start as she sped up into the network of branches. Bekko could hardly see her as he worked his way through the leafy treetops. He didn't mind, though; he had a plan for a new route that was going to bring him closer to her further up the hill. Head up, he jumped swiftly and decisively from branch to branch. Every landing was safe and strong.

Ahead of him, Suki was flying by her fingertips. She had a few lucky grabs and some dramatic misses, regaining height quickly every time she dropped. For a while she skimmed along so quickly it seemed as if she wasn't even touching the trees, then she reached in vain for a high branch. Clasping a desperate handful of leaves she tumbled into space, bracing herself to roll as she hit the ground. The fall winded her; she sat up groggily, battling for breath and slightly dizzy. At first, she wondered if she was hallucinating as a huge creature bombed towards her through the forest, but a volley of barking and the sight of big, sharp teeth convinced her that this was both real and dangerous. Rousing herself, she swung into the nearest tree just in time, whisking her tail away from the dripping jaws of the savage-looking animal. From the safety of her branch she stared down at it in confusion, as it reared onto its back legs, snapping and

snarling. It was not as big as Kuma but it was still bigger than either herself or Bekko. It seemed to be a solid mass of muscle and teeth, certainly not looking to chat or make friends. On the contrary, its whole mission seemed to be to use those teeth to grab hold of her . . . why? Was it hungry? Was it angry? She couldn't tell. She had never seen anything like it before.

Higher up the hill, Bekko reached the silver fir and quickly marked his win on the bark at the top. Now he was only two points behind Suki! He sat proudly, looking across at the volcano while waiting for Suki's arrival. When she didn't arrive straight away, he was a little puzzled. Then he heard the barking noise and became very worried indeed. Cautiously, he made his way towards the sound, staying high off the ground. Through the leaves he saw the animal jumping up at a tree, and he was relieved to see Suki safely in the higher branches. He took his time to reach her via a network of careful jumps and they huddled together, puzzling over what they saw.

'I think it's a dog,' Bekko said. 'We don't have them here but I saw them in a book once. Gimandesh has all sorts of dogs. Not all as big as this one, though. What does it want?'

'Apart from to eat us?' Suki shrugged. 'No idea. Do you want to ask it?'

'No thanks! But I wonder how it got here? How weird!'

'Are we trapped? Do you think it would follow us? I hope not!' Suki peered down at the dog, which glared back, growling. Suddenly, however, a powerful whistling sound penetrated the forest. Immediately the dog's ears lifted, its head turned and it dashed away towards the volcano.

'It was summoned!' Bekko raised his eyebrows. 'Do you think it's a slave of some kind?'

'No idea! Let's go after it! Maybe there's more! We should find out! We didn't look for more clouds either! Come on!' Suki was clearly excited about investigating this.

But Bekko felt their secret mission should not be a secret any more.

'Suki,' he said, hesitantly. 'I think we need to go back. We should tell Kuma about the dog. And if we go after it now we might be in danger.'

'Danger? Pah. We can always climb a tree,' Suki replied scornfully. 'We're supposed to be warriors. Warriors aren't afraid of danger.'

'Actually,' Bekko corrected her, 'warriors feel fear but still take action. When necessary. We don't need to go after the dog. In fact, I think we need to tell Kuma.'

'But we could find out more! Then tell him everything. Come on! We don't really know anything yet,' Suki pleaded.

Fara's words rang in Bekko's ears. Would Suki respect him for having a different opinion? He had to try.

'Look, Suki, I know you are excited about this. I am too, although to be truthful I'm also a bit scared. But it might be serious trouble, and we are only students. Don't you think Kuma should check on this with us? He would be safe from the dog because he's bigger. And he will know what to do.'

'Oh, Bekko! I really want to go look! It won't take long, then we can go back, I promise!' she said. He looked at her face, seeing how reluctant she was to return. Fine. Then he had no choice.

'You can go on, if you like. But I'm going back. Sorry, Suki. But I think it is the right thing to do.' It was really hard for him to say, and she recognized his determination, even though it was not what she wanted. And she gave in.

'OK, OK, you're right, Sensei Sensible! Let's go and tell Kuma. He would be pretty mad with us if we got eaten by a dog. Come on then.' She bumped his shoulder affectionately, and he blinked a couple of times, feeling he had done something quite brave. They turned together to return to Senshi Castle, then froze in disbelief as the ground shook beneath them. It wasn't enough to make them wobble on their feet, but it was definitely more than Suki had felt in the garden. Behind them, the volcano looked innocent enough, but a tell-tale thread of cloud was winding its way up out of the crater.

'Wow! That is definitely not imagination!' Bekko exclaimed, clearly both fascinated and horrified. 'I'm sure my library book didn't predict any rumbles like that.'

'I don't think Mount Niru has read your library book, Bekko.

Time to get Kuma here. Race you back!'
She got a good head start while Bekko
watched the thin cloud blow away across
the sea, then he shook himself into action
and set off after her at top speed.

CHAPTER FIVE

When they reached Kuma, they told
their story as quickly as possible. Kuma
seemed quite alarmed, both about the
dog and about the rumbles in the ground.
He agreed with Bekko that there should
be no danger from any eruption, but that
it was peculiar for the volcano to be active
earlier than expected.

'Where did the dog go?' he asked them.
Of this, they were both absolutely sure.

'It went towards Mount Niru.'
Suki was firm, and Bekko nodded his agreement.

'Definitely,' he confirmed. 'And it went fast. I'd almost say it looked scared. Did you think that too, Suki?'

'Hard to say,' she frowned. 'Yes, maybe, but I don't know what dogs normally look like.'

'I don't like the sound of any of it.' Kuma frowned seriously. 'Yet it could be just some random rumbles and a dog from a trader ship.'

'What about whatever called the dog, though?' Bekko pointed out. 'There's something more going on.'

'Good point,' said Kuma, reaching for

his armour. 'You can show me where the dog went and we'll see if there is anything suspicious. Then we'll make a report for Sensei Rika. She will need to know what we've seen.'

When Kuma was ready Suki and Bekko leapt up on his back. They felt like proper warriors, protecting the Shanti Islands. Suki was thrilled to be heading for potential danger. Bekko was nervous, but he felt safe with Kuma and Suki, no matter what they were facing. At least they were facing it together.

The journey flew past at Kuma's speed, and before long they had made it to the foot of Mount Niru. The volcano

towered over them, its steep sides laced with narrow paths and overhanging vegetation. Low plumes of smoke formed a distinct cloud over the ragged edges of the open peak. Had there been more rumbles? At close range, the smell of gas was extremely unpleasant.

'Ugh, gross!' Suki pinched her nose and stuck out her tongue. 'I don't even want to breathe!'

Bekko was trying hard not to make a fuss. 'All volcanoes smell like that. It's the sulphur gases escaping. You will get used to it.'

'It feels like it's sticking to my throat. Yuck!'

'We have to focus on what's important, Suki, however bad the stink! What's the plan, Kuma?'

'We'll start by scouting round the base to see if we can spot anything unusual.' Kuma indicated the rough path that circled the volcano.

'Something unusual like . . . that?' Bekko pointed through the trees to a distant line of small creatures marching towards the same path.

'Are those meerkats?' Suki asked, puzzled. 'I've never seen them so organized! They're normally running all over the place.'

'Exactly.' Bekko was staring at the marching line as it tramped forwards mechanically. 'They look more like ants! And are they carrying something?'

Kuma nodded. 'Yes, Bekko, I think I see a box or packet over their shoulders, is that what you mean?'

'Yes, all identical. This is spooky. They look like they're under a spell. Can we get closer without being seen?'

'You two can sneak in far better than I can. I'll head up to that ridge over there and see if I can get a better view of the south side. Let's meet back here. It's all very peculiar; I've no idea what's going on but I really don't like it.'

Suki and Bekko moved expertly

through the undergrowth in the direction
taken by the meerkats. They didn't need
to speak to each other as they stayed
shoulder to shoulder, both keeping
a sharp eye out for any dangers or
obstacles. They swung up into the low
branches of a tree overlooking the path
and they saw that the marching meerkats
were disappearing into the base of the
volcano.

'The caves!' Bekko whispered. 'They're using the old lava tunnels. But why?'

Mount Niru had a web of tunnels around its surface created by lava flows in long-ago eruptions. Suki and Bekko had never been permitted to explore these, although Sensei had once taken them into one of the caves on the edge of the tunnel network just to show them how hot, dark, and unpleasant they really were.

'Also, can you smell charcoal?' Bekko had his nose up in the air, sniffing suspiciously.

'Are you kidding? Your nose is ridiculous!' Suki couldn't smell anything except the disgusting sulphur that hung in the air all around Mount Niru. Charcoal? Another bizarre clue, if Bekko was correct.

'Let's go nearer to the tunnels,' she suggested. 'Whatever those meerkats are doing, their eyes look completely blank. If they are being enchanted then I don't think they are going to notice us even if we're in front of them.'

'Maybe, Suki, but whatever is controlling them must be really dangerous. And don't forget that crazy dog. We have to be careful.'

'Agreed. Let's see which cave they are

going into, then go back to Kuma. Deal?'

'Deal.'

As it happened, their decision was a good one. As they crept round the path towards the caves, not only could they see exactly where the stream of brainwashed animals was headed, but they saw a break in the line. A meerkat had tripped and fallen, hitting its head on the rocky entrance to the tunnels. The others appeared not to notice and continued their automatic steps into the cave beyond.

The meerkat lay unconscious about ten metres away from their hiding place.

'Let's grab him!' Suki said excitedly, eyeing up the distance. Bekko winced. He was torn between the risk and the reward. No doubt it would help them to know what the meerkats were doing, if this injured creature could tell them anything. But would Kuma think it was too dangerous to break cover and run out? What if they were seen by whoever (or whatever) was controlling this relentless line of upright soldiers? He came to a brave decision.

'Let me do it,' he said to Suki.

'What? No, I should do it. I am faster than you.'

'Yes, I know. That's why. If I get into trouble you need to race to get Kuma. Promise me you'll do that. We have no idea what is happening here but it has to be something powerful. And that dog is around somewhere.'

Suki could see from Bekko's face that he was absolutely determined. Even though she didn't want to agree with him again, she could see that his idea made sense. And it looked perfectly safe, no sign of anyone else except for the unnatural plodding line, which seemed endless.

'Right. Go then. Good luck!' They bumped fists and Bekko took a last scan of the area to check all was clear.

He crouched on the branch, composed himself then dropped decisively and sprinted to the sprawled body by the cave.

—❁—

Up on the ridge, Kuma had been disturbed by the view of the south side of the volcano. More meerkats were carrying their cargo into the tunnels. That was bad. There was also a line flowing out of a different tunnel, but these meerkats had no boxes. Maybe that was worse! Whatever was going into the caves was not coming out. What could it be? He was desperate to look at the boxes and see what was piling up in the base of the volcano. How could he

get hold of one without being seen? He continued to ponder this while keeping lookout and waiting for Suki and Bekko to return. He spotted some movement in the undergrowth; were the student warriors losing their touch? They should be able to creep up without being seen! All became clear when Suki and Bekko emerged from the bushes. Bekko was carrying an unconscious meerkat. Suki was carrying . . . a small wooden box.

Firstly, they attended to the injured animal.

'I think it is only his head that's hurt.' Bekko showed Kuma where he had tried to stop the bleeding with a strip of cloth from his jacket.

'OK, I will check it out. Open the box, but do it carefully!'

Suki and Bekko prised off the wooden lid to find the box was packed full of a black powder. It smelt like . . . charcoal. Suki looked up, alarmed.

'Kuma! They're packing the volcano with explosives!'

'I don't want to scare anyone,' Bekko said tentatively, 'but if every box under the volcano has this much powder . . .'

'It could trigger a massive eruption.' Kuma finished the sentence for him.

'Why are the meerkats doing this? It truly doesn't make sense. They live here.

They wouldn't want an eruption.' Bekko looked over the ridge at the relentless line delivering its deadly boxes.

'What do we do, Kuma?' Suki's voice was edged with panic and urgency.

'I'm going to Senshi Castle for reinforcements,' said Kuma. 'I'll take our meerkat friend to Fara for some medical help. You two must stay here; stay hidden and keep watch.'

'Of course.' Suki was glad they were being left on lookout.

Bekko's hand strayed to a warm round pebble deep in his pocket and he thought wistfully about organizing his stones in the safety of his own room. Still, as Sensei Rika would say, skills must be tested to be real. This was very real.

'OK, Kuma. You can rely on us.'

'I know I can. And I will be back as fast as I can.'

Solemnly, they helped secure the groaning meerkat to Kuma's back, gave their friend a big hug, and watched him gallop off towards the castle.

'Where should we wait?' Suki asked Bekko. 'We need to be able to see well without being seen. Maybe higher up towards the crater we could get the best view and keep out of sight under the bushes?'

'I'm nervous, Suki. What if we see that dog? What if that dog sees us? Do you think the dog is making the meerkats carry the powder?'

'I don't think a dog could do that, Bekko. I think it has to be something a lot more powerful. I bet Sensei Rika will know. I just hope she gets here in time! That rumble we heard before, and the charcoal you could smell . . . don't you think this means that explosions have already started? How many would it take before a proper eruption happens?'

'I was wondering that myself,' Bekko admitted. 'Just a guess, but I reckon you would need several small explosions around the base to make it really unstable, and then a big one to set it off. We know there have been at least two already; I'm guessing probably a lot more.'

Suki's stomach lurched at the thought. So it was a race, but they didn't know how much time they had left. Even stranger, they didn't know who they were racing! Together, they made their way up towards the crater's edge, creeping under the bushes rather than leaping from tree to tree. As they got closer to the top they spotted a rocky outcrop with some bushes underneath. Surely this would be the best lookout point? It was a short run but seemed worth the risk. Suki led the way as they scurried across to the scrubby gorse bushes and dived underneath. Bekko flopped down, relieved they had a safe shelter.

Then Suki tapped Bekko's arm twice. This was their signal for emergency.

'No sudden movements,' she mouthed, with complete calm and an almost Chan-like stillness. The alarm in her eyes was the only thing that showed the danger they had fallen into. Bekko resisted the temptation to jump up, instead very

slowly turning his head to look where Suki indicated. Above them, on the very edge of the crater a colossal bird had landed. Folding vast wings, it preened itself with its huge, cruel beak. Bekko and Suki stared at each other and then back to the giant bird. Suki thought back to the cards from Kuma's floor and wrote in the dust with a shaky finger: 'Tengu?'

Bekko wanted to cry. He could see she was right: it must be a tengu. All birds were enemies of the islanders but the size and appearance of this one was unmistakable. And, just like on Bekko's card, it carried both the traditional magical objects: a staff of incantations to enchant and control other animals, and a large fan for whipping up powerful winds.

Suki felt sick and terrified. Here was their explanation for the spellbound meerkats. Evidently this evil creature was at the heart of the mystery. They heard the tengu mutter low clicking and humming sounds as he drew lines

in the air with the long staff. He was so wrapped up in the spell that he did not notice the two monkeys crouching in the bushes.

Suki and Bekko had never been in a more perilous situation. Any movement might give them away, yet they urgently needed to escape to warn Sensei Rika of the danger. But this day of surprises was about to take another horrible turn. Through the bush they spied a massive mandrill approaching up the hill, dragging another unconscious meerkat by its neck. The tengu seemed annoyed but not surprised to see him.

'Jirugi! What's wrong with that one?'

'I think it knocked itself out on the

tunnel ceiling. They're not too clever when they're far away from your control. They seem to get more confused. I think you should come down lower. Only one more small explosion to go before the big one, after all.'

'It's not for you to decide where I choose to stand, Jirugi! Do you think you can handle this spell better than I? No one can do that!'

'Calm down! It was only a suggestion. I'm sure you know best. As long as you get the job done, I don't care how you do it.'

The tengu snapped, 'You monkeys are all the same! So full of your own importance.'

Suki and Bekko heard Jirugi snarl.

'Look, Ikoto. Don't push me. We have a deal. You'll get control of the Shanti Islands. I'll get my revenge. Then we can leave each other alone.'

There was a tense silence. Peeking through the bush, Suki could see the tengu stick his beak up in the air, and glare furiously at Jirugi. Jirugi seemed completely unaffected by this, but when he spoke again, he sounded less hostile.

'Shall we check on the west side fuses? The last trigger explosion should be ready to detonate on schedule.'

'You can do so if you wish. I intend to go lower and make sure the meerkats are doing their job properly.' They could hear the big monkey sigh, but he did not point out that had been his idea in the first place.

There was a grunt of farewell, and a swoosh of wings. A shadow passed over their hiding place as the tengu swung into the air. They saw Jirugi hauling the meerkat along as he disappeared around the crater's edge and out of sight. Only

then did they start to breathe again. Suki realized she had been pressing herself back into the thorny gorse without even feeling the spikes.

'Down to the ridge?' Bekko whispered, shakily. Did she nod or was her head just wobbling with shock? Quickly and quietly, they sneaked back down the hill, desperate to pass on their knowledge to Kuma and whoever he brought back from Senshi Castle.

CHAPTER 6

Once they were safely back behind the ridge, Suki and Bekko were able to talk about what they had discovered. One thing Suki didn't understand was how Jirugi expected an eruption to wipe out the inhabitants of the islands.

'The islands have always been safe before!' she said, puzzled. 'When Mount Niru erupts the wind blows the lava and ash south over the sea, not north over the islands.'

'Well yes, Suki, that is true. But remember the tengu doesn't just hypnotize weaker animals . . .'

'Oh no.' Suki's eyes widened sharply. 'It's the fan. Tengus can control the winds.'

'Exactly. With a strong wind blasting lava and ash to the north, who knows how bad it could be? And we don't know how long until the big explosion is due. Oh, hurry up Kuma!'

At that very moment, they felt a vibration in the earth. It grew suddenly, with a series of deep, rippling rumbles. Trees quivered. Dust was shaken up like a shallow mist. And the smell of

charcoal wove its way into the sulphurous
air. Clearly, the west tunnels had
been blasted. Bekko imagined the lava
cauldron deep in the crater like one of
Fara's pots . . . bubbling and spattering its
boiling liquid against the walls . . . rising
. . . waiting for a big enough trigger to
launch high into the sky. He shuddered.

Suki pulled his arm and pointed
towards the coastal path.

'Look,' she said, sounding relieved. 'I can see bears.'

From their hideout they could make out two big guard bears galloping at breakneck speed. Kuma led the way and Priya, Sensei Rika's bear, was behind. Bekko could see both bears carried a Kuro Warrior, dressed in battle robes and carrying a long staff. Rika was easily recognizable, but her majestic companion, urging the bear onwards, long hair streaming behind him as they galloped along . . . ?

'Suki, it's Chan! Look at him go!'

'Wow! I've never seen him in battle gear. I don't think I've ever seen him outside the castle.' Amazed, Suki nearly

forgot to be scared. However, the anxiety over the imminent eruption quickly overcame her again. They set off to meet the warriors and tell them everything they had discovered.

Kuma and Priya skidded to a halt, panting, as Bekko and Suki ran out in front of them, waving wildly.

'Jirugi is back! He's the one trying to set off the volcano!' Suki's words had an immediate effect on the warriors. Chan and Rika jumped down from the bears, whose first reaction to hearing Jirugi's name was to snarl and look around warily.

'Jirugi.' Chan shook his head sadly. 'I

was afraid he would be involved with this mischief.'

Bekko rushed into the worst part of the news. 'He's got a tengu helping him. He's used a spell to control the meerkats and stack up the explosives around the volcano. They've got one big explosion left, and it's going to be really bad!'

'A tengu!' Rika looked angry. 'Loathsome, arrogant creatures. Ideal companion for Jirugi. Despicable.'

'We think it will use the wind fan to blow the lava and ash north over the

islands,' added Suki quickly. 'It could be terrible! Not just for Senshi but maybe all the Shanti Islands. What can we do?'

Sensei Rika turned to Priya.

'This is worse than I thought. Much as I'd like to have you with me, I need you to go back to Senshi and raise the alarm in case we don't make it in time to stop the blast. Evacuate everyone to the vaults in Silla. It's the best chance to keep everyone safe. Go well.'

Priya wasted no time with goodbyes; she simply

bowed her head politely and set off.

'Do we know where the fuses are for the explosion?' Kuma asked. 'And any idea how long we've got to stop it?'

'We can assume that Jirugi will be a safe distance from the blast. He will have left time to get away,' Chan's calm voice helped Suki to think clearly.

'I think they will be sending meerkats,' she said. 'They don't care if any get hurt or killed. Jirugi was checking the west side fuses before the explosion there, though, so maybe he would be checking the south ones before Ikoto sends them in?' Her suggestion made sense.

Sensei Rika nodded decisively. 'Right. We split up then. There are two access points for the southern tunnels. Chan, could you take Kuma with you to investigate the tunnels on the far side? See if you can block off the opening. Bekko, Suki, you're with me. We're going back to where you found that meerkat. You can help to stop the meerkats, but if we find Jirugi you leave him to me. Is that clear?'

'Yes, Sensei.'

'Right. Good luck everyone. Let's go.'

As she hurried towards the caves with Sensei Rika, Suki could see Kuma galloping away up the hill, Chan silhouetted against the skyline. Beside her, Bekko was stumbling along with his head low and his hands in his pockets.

His breathing was rapid and panicky and he looked as frightened as she felt.

'Are you OK?' she asked quietly, even though she knew it was a stupid question.

'Being brave is when you're scared but you do the right thing anyway,' he stuttered. Suki wasn't sure if he was telling her, or telling himself. Either way, she squeezed his arm with as much comfort as she could manage and braced herself for whatever was to come.

The entrance to the cave was in a small clearing, surrounded by trees and bushes on three sides. Above the cave itself, there was a mixture of rocks and scrub rising steeply up the side of the volcano. From

their vantage point across the clearing
they could see the opening which had
been busy with meerkats earlier. Now,
however, the clearing was full of strange
statues. A battalion of meerkats stood
in neat rows, each staring ahead blankly.
Glazed and immobile, they held unlit

torches.

'They're
waiting, which is a
relief.' Sensei Rika
murmured. 'Jirugi
must still be in the
tunnels. Do you
see that fire?'

Suki had spotted it too; a small bonfire
burned strongly by the cave's entrance.

'Yes,' she said. 'Ready for lighting the
torches. The fuses must be set to allow
time for him to get away?'

'Indeed. And will probably be lit from
both sides if the black powder heap is as
big as we think. I wonder what Chan and
Kuma have found?'

Chan and Kuma had, in fact, found
an identical scene; spellbound soldiers
waiting for orders. Firstly they worked to
put out the fire, Kuma digging rapidly to
create a pile of earth which Chan used to
smother the flames.

Kuma poked about inside the tunnel's entrance, looking for a way to block it up.

He called out from inside the cave.

'Chan? There's some rubble in here and a boulder I think I can roll to cover the entrance.'

'That should keep them out. But it will also shut you in. Can you find your way through the tunnel to the other exit? Remember, Jirugi might also be somewhere down there, unless he has already left.'

Kuma began to dig around the boulder to free it up. 'I think this will work,' he said, rocking it to test how deeply it was buried. 'It won't take long. I'll catch you up through the caves.'

'Good. I shall return to Sensei Rika. Our mission is far from over, and the action is not going to be here.'

Sensei Rika, Suki, and Bekko stood by the entrance to the cave. Without a bear to dig earth, it was not so easy for them to put out a fire. Although small, it was well-established and burning strongly.

'Nearest water is way back near the main path,' Bekko said. 'And we have no buckets, even if we had time to run back there.'

'No need, Bekko.' Sensei Rika had a different solution. 'If we take away their torches, they won't be able to light the fuses anyway. With all three of us working together, we should be able to do it quickly.'

But it was already too late.

'Ohhhhh, I don't think you will.' A nasty voice boomed out from the darkness. 'I think you will stay exactly where you are!'

From inside the tunnel there was a deep growling. Then three snarling dogs rushed out. Their savage eyes were terrifying; their huge teeth looked sharp and ready to rip.

Ready to leap, they crouched . . . then . . .

'WAIT!'

The dogs froze instantly, maintaining eye contact and growling, but obedient

to the commanding voice. Behind them,
Jirugi swaggered out of the cave and
bowed to Sensei Rika, very sarcastically.

'Ah, Rika! Welcome to my party. I'm
certain it's going to go with a bang!'

CHAPTER SEVEN

Sensei Rika didn't flinch, ignoring the dogs snarling at their feet. Suki and Bekko tried to imitate her proud stance, although they couldn't help their eyes flickering between the dogs—their sharp-looking teeth!—and Jirugi, whose scornful gaze was fixed on Sensei Rika.

'Rika!' He spat her name. 'You don't seem to have changed much. I can't say I've missed your annoying habit of showing up when you're not wanted.'

Sensei Rika replied calmly, her voice firm and clear.

'This, Jirugi? This is what you choose to do with your power? Invade and destroy? Think about all the innocent creatures living here. They are doing no harm. Why would you kill them?'

Her words only seemed to rile Jirugi.

'Power, ha! You took my power away from me. I want revenge! I don't care about your "innocent creatures" and they don't care about me. I'm going to wipe them out and let the birds move in. Ikoto is ready and waiting for his kingdom.'

'Ah yes, your tengu friend. How low you've sunk for this petty revenge! And I see you've got dogs working for you.'

Suki could tell that Sensei had a poor opinion of dogs. 'I guess you couldn't get monkeys on your side. At least dogs will fight for you without asking intelligent questions.'

'I don't need monkeys. And I don't need your opinion, either! My dogs do exactly as I tell them. No need to have a stupid meeting and chat about what's fair. I decide!'

At that moment, Sensei Rika's stance changed. Her shoulders dropped. Her voice sounded sad and defeated.

'Well we're outnumbered here and we're obviously too late to stop you. I will surrender if you let these young warriors go free.'

Suki could not contain herself.

'We're not leaving you, Sensei!' she burst out passionately. 'Never!'

'You will do as I tell you. Now is not the time for playful heroics, Suki.'

But even Bekko was determined to disobey. He looked at Sensei Rika and shook his head hard, with tears in his eyes.

And . . . she winked at him. She winked at him! What was going on? She must have a plan! Was it some kind of delay?

Jirugi enjoyed her words.

'You cannot save these monkeys, and you cannot save anyone! You've failed. Today, and always! You will bow before me and die as my prisoner, Sensei Rika.

You were Guardian of Senshi! Now Senshi will burn. Lay down your weapons and get on your knees, Warrior Monkeys!'

Suki and Bekko were again puzzled by how swiftly and meekly Sensei Rika knelt. She placed her long staff flat in front of her as she touched her head to the ground before Jirugi. Suki felt cold despair trickle into her heart as she and Bekko knelt too. Jirugi smiled a satisfied, ugly grin as he stood triumphant over them. Bekko, however, had now seen what Sensei Rika had seen: a stealthy robed warrior descending the hill above the cave entrance. His heartbeat accelerated and his stomach was doing somersaults as he knelt quickly and did his best to pretend

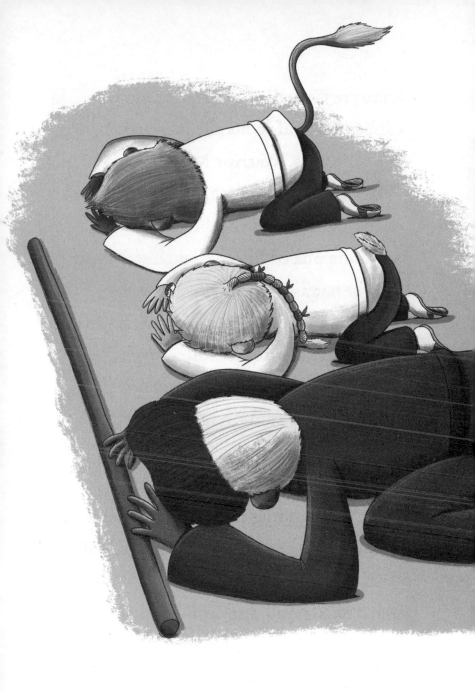

an expression of utter defeat. He had to stop himself from cheering, and elbowing Suki to share what he had seen. Where there was Chan, there was still a chance!

A moment of heavy silence stretched out as Jirugi soaked up his victory, gloating over the prisoners. Bekko glued his eyes to the ground, feeling his heart thumping. He was determined not to give away the approach of Chan, who had prowled to a low stance on the top of the cave, just over Jirugi's head. Jirugi was entirely focused on his prisoners as he raised a foot to kick Rika. In the instant that he swung his leg there was a bloodcurdling scream—

'BANZAIIIIIIIIIIIII!'—as both Rika and Chan exploded into movement simultaneously. Rika rolled to the side, grabbing her staff and knocking Jirugi off his feet. Chan had landed like a panther and was now fighting all three dogs. He barely seemed to move, deflecting their attacks with lightning-fast manipulations of his staff. Rika and Jirugi bounded back to their feet immediately and began to fight for control of her staff.

Bekko had also rolled out of the way but now could not see Suki. Had she run into the tunnel? Maybe that was the best place to go. One of the dogs broke free from the battle and surged towards him, snarling. He had no more time to think;

no way to get to the safety of a tree; no
choice but to turn and dive into the caves
as fast as he could move. The dog chased
him into the tunnel, terrifying him with
its barking. The daylight gave out very
quickly, leaving him stumbling into the
darkness. Was it his imagination, or had
the dog abandoned its pursuit? Had it
returned to the fight? Maybe it had gone
after Suki instead; oh, where was Suki?
Was she hiding somewhere safe or was
she ahead of him? He didn't dare stop
and look back. Then, in his panic, he
tripped and hit his head as he fell to the
rocky floor and blacked out.

Suki was not hiding somewhere safe. At

first she had rolled quickly behind the bushes to get away from the dogs. As the battle in front of the tunnels continued, she looked around to see where Bekko had gone but couldn't see him anywhere. She decided to climb a tree to see if she could spot him without being seen herself. She hoped the dogs couldn't reach her there if they saw her. From the branches she could see the fighting, but no Bekko.

At first, the battle seized her attention entirely. She had never seen such skills shown under pressure. She could immediately see the power and skill of Jirugi: yet he and Sensei were still matching each other blow for blow. She

164

saw one grabbing hold of the stick, then
the other would dodge, twist, and disarm.
Jirugi was stronger; Sensei was faster. At
any other time Suki would have wanted
to keep watching in pure admiration
but her brain was ticking with urgency,
demanding she do something.

What should she do? Without Bekko,
she decided her best action would be to
go and help the warriors if she could,
even as a distraction. Maybe she could
help Chan fight one of those dogs. She
couldn't just sit in the tree and watch.
However, as she turned to climb down,
her eye was caught by activity behind
the whirling battle of monkeys and dogs.
The line of meerkats had begun to move.

Whatever was happening with Jirugi,
Ikoto was going to continue with his part
of the plan, whether Jirugi had made his
escape or not! They were entering the
volcano base. And—ohhhhhhh!—they
were dipping their torches into the flames
as they went. This was every kind of bad
news! Everyone else was too busy to see.
Her thoughts were suddenly swarming
like bees; confusion overcoming her.
In the noise of the battle, she felt
desperately alone.

Back in the tunnel, Bekko woke fuzzily.
He opened his eyes. Then he shut them
again. Then opened them again. It was so,
so dark! Then he remembered where he

was and felt himself begin to panic; throat tight, lungs heaving. Grabbing hold of his swirling anxiety he squashed it into his belly with breaths that were ragged at first, becoming deeper and more controlled as he gained focus. He tried to imagine that he was back in the training hall, blindfolded. Sensei would help him to think with his senses. He listened . . . the sounds of the fight continued in the distance. What did that tell him? Where the exit was! But it was also where the dogs were, where Jirugi was . . . maybe he should be looking for another way out. It was so hot, and impossibly dark!

He felt his way carefully upright, ready to start feeling his way along. It felt better to be standing. He had even started imagining light. Because didn't that look like light coming towards him? A row of torches, coming closer. Was he being rescued? Then as the line of flames continued to approach he suddenly realized it was the meerkats on their way to light the fuses. Nothing stood between the torches and the black powder now, apart from him. There were so many of them! And he was just one small monkey; overwhelmed and afraid. He thought desperately about all his friends who might die if they did not stop the eruption. Then he thought about Fara. 'How do you eat an elephant, Bekko?' 'One bite at a time.' He thought

to himself. 'Can I stop just one meerkat?'
And he knew that he could. He stood in
the middle of the tunnel ready to take the
first torch, then keep taking them until
he could take no more.

Back in the tree, Suki wrestled with
indecision. Think, Suki, think! There was
no point in following the meerkats, they
were too far ahead. What could she do?
And then it hit her. The key was Ikoto;
the tengu. Find Ikoto. He had activated
the meerkats. He had the fan to steer
the wind. Where was he? Her anxious
brain rattled with useless thoughts and
she didn't know which way to go. This
was no good! She saw Chan still fighting

across the clearing. He would know what to do. He would know because he would be calm.

Suki sat in the tree and did the hardest thing she had ever tried. Ignoring the battle on one side and the meerkats on the other, she focused on a single leaf moving in the breeze and breathed deeply. How could she save Senshi? The answer dropped into her brain; she knew it was right. And she set off up the hill, away from all the action. If the tengu was waiting to direct the lava then he must be at the top of the volcano. Nowhere else would do. She sped up Mount Niru, leaping lightly from rock to rock and swinging through the trees. Her fear and confusion had all given way to the clear purpose in her mind.

Bekko's fear and confusion had also been brushed aside as he ambushed each meerkat and wrestled for the torches one at a time. The first few had been easy enough—the creatures were smaller than him and they were too immersed in the spell to fight back properly. However, as they continued to march onwards, Bekko was standing by an ever-growing bonfire of discarded torches and the tunnel was full of meerkats trying to continue towards the powder kegs. They bumped into the walls, into each other . . . and into a large brown bear making his way towards the light. Bekko couldn't believe his ears when he heard Kuma's voice.

'Hey, Bekko. You look busy! Need a hand?'

CHAPTER EIGHT

Approaching the edge of the crater, Suki slowed down and began to move more carefully. She knew her only chance of success was to sneak up and surprise the tengu. Not only was he huge and powerful, he could also fly, so could easily escape if he saw her. Luckily for her he had plenty on his mind. She could hear his irritable voice long before she saw him perched on a ledge jutting out inside the volcano. He had his back to her, low down to her left. She crept over the edge of the crater and edged closer to him, hoping to hear what he was saying.

'Useless monkey! I should have known better than to trust him! Serve him right if he doesn't get away. It's time!'

He brandished the staff of incantation and began to chant: 'Servant whirlwind, hear me. Obey your master! Grow!'

Suki felt the air around them begin to move, slowly at first, but then the breeze spiralled, gathering force and height. She could see that it was already sucking in debris: branches, loose stones, and earth were drawn in as the tengu began to move his whirlwind along the edge of the crater, directing it with his fan and using the stick of enchantment to increase its size with every line of his spell. Suki's throat seemed to close and her chest felt squeezed with worry. She looked at the distance between herself and the tengu. Was it further than she could jump? She realized it didn't much matter. She was going to try anyway.

She shook her legs and looked across the gap. For a moment she glanced down; that was a mistake. This time there was no cliff to slide on or bushes to break her fall. But her training was not for stealing nuts and annoying squirrels. Her training was to be a warrior and protect the islands. Her training was for now. She

breathed. She focused. And she jumped.

From the base of the volcano it must have been an amazing sight to see a tiny monkey silhouetted against the sky: an airborne arc reaching into space. Time slowed down for Suki as she stretched out for the tengu's staff. For Ikoto it was a huge shock: a monkey suddenly dropped out of the sky onto his shoulder, grabbing his stick. It was not enough of a shock to make him let go, however, but with a surge of determination and desperation Suki would not be shaken off. She didn't have a great knowledge of stick fighting but she did have extremely sharp teeth. She bit him as hard as she could.

'Aaaaaargh!' Ikoto cursed furiously and let go. Suki took the staff and leapt out of reach before he could recover. He gathered himself to fly after her but it was too late. Reaching the jagged edge of the crater, she threw all her strength into bending the staff until ...CRACK! a thunderous snapping noise echoed around the inside of the volcano. Looking up, Suki saw the whirlwind disintegrating instantly, and as if he too had been snapped, Ikoto staggered and fell. The broken staff had broken his spell, and his spirit. His bravado and importance vanished with the wind. For a moment, Suki was afraid he was coming after her as he lurched back to his feet, but to her

intense relief he flapped into the air with
unsteady wings. She watched him departing;
with his head down and not a backward
glance. Perhaps he was unable to face the
humiliation of being beaten by a very small,
very brave, Warrior Monkey.

In the tunnel, the meerkats awoke with a jump. Most of them dropped their torches with surprise and they began to chatter busily to each other, checking on their friends.

Kuma and Bekko hugged each other in relief.

'What happened, Kuma?' Bekko asked.

But Kuma had no idea. All they knew was that the spell appeared to be broken. Now instead of stopping the meerkats, they began to shepherd them towards out of the caves. Kuma took time to reassure them, even though both he and Bekko were bursting to know what had happened to their friends.

Bekko was bruised and burned in places but his main thought was still Suki. As they left the tunnels the light was blinding, but he could see just Sensei Rika, Chan, and one dog in the clearing. No Suki. And no Jirugi.

Sensei Rika rushed towards them.

'What happened in the tunnels? How did you break the spell?'

Kuma clapped Bekko on the shoulder.

'This young warrior did his best to stop a whole army on his own, Sensei. But I don't know why the spell was broken. What happened here?'

'That coward, Jirugi!' she grimaced. 'When he could see he was losing, he chose to throw one of his dogs at me to cause a distraction. I think its leg is broken. He and the other two dogs escaped together in the chaos.'

Chan was holding the dog gently; trying to calm it in order to splint its leg.

'Where's Suki?' he asked. 'Has no one seen her?'

'I lost her when the fight started' Bekko explained. 'I thought she must be in the tunnels but there was no sign of her anywhere.' The worry made his voice wobble.

'May I go back in the tunnels and look for her, Sensei?'

'Well, you could do,' smiled Sensei Rika, 'but I think you might start by looking over there.'

Coming down the path towards them was a small, tired monkey with a broken magical staff and a big story to tell. Kuma and Bekko ran to meet her with tears like raindrops. Suki's eyes lit up when she saw they were both safe and smiling, despite the tears.

She leaned against Kuma. Funny how she felt so much older for all she had been through, yet the overwhelming feeling of safety made her feel like a sleepy toddler. 'Can we go home now?'

'I think that would be fair enough,' Sensei Rika laughed. 'You are both VERY late, the bell for dinner must have sounded hours ago! What am I going to do with you?'

Chan chuckled too. 'I have a suggestion, Sensei Rika, if I may?'

'Go ahead!'

'Let's make them cadets, shall we? Their stick fighting certainly needs a bit of training, and perhaps they have shown they can be trusted with some responsibility.'

Tired as they were, Bekko and Suki's delight shone in their faces. Cadets! Weapons training! Kuma beamed at them proudly, mirroring their own happiness.

'Excellent plan, thank you!' Sensei Rika agreed. 'Now, you two red belts, get yourselves back to Senshi with Kuma. Chan and I will check all is safe in the

tunnels and bring this poor dog back
for some first aid. And perhaps . . . a
celebration. What do you think?'

The party was the biggest ever known
at Senshi Castle. Chan mixed some of
the black powder to make fireworks,
which lit up the sky over the islands.
Fara created spectacular fruity sushi.
The excitement, the crowds, the music,
and the happiness would be a bright
memory for those who attended.

Some, however, preferred to step
back and celebrate in their own way.
Leaving Kang, Nita, and Lili in an
acrobatic dance-off, Suki slid quietly

out of the hubbub and found herself
pacing towards the water garden. There
sat Bekko lining up some smooth
stones in rows of size and colour. She
settled next to him companionably and
they sat together watching the stones
grow.

THE RULES OF THE WARRIOR MONKEYS

COURTESY –Treating others as we would like to be treated: with respect and kindness. There is no such thing as a shy warrior.

HUMILITY – The warrior's journey is not measured against others. Sometimes you will be faster, sometimes slower, but there is always a new challenge.

INTEGRITY – To know the difference between right and wrong and to choose the right path. Warriors do not steal, do not speak ill of friends, and they take responsibility for their own actions.

Acknowledgements

Firstly, I would like to thank Sensei Rob King whose firm belief in the power of the life lessons of martial arts has been a huge inspiration in my life and work. For critical reading of the manuscript I would like to thank Steve Chapman (comma controller), Joseph Mutch (action activist) and my children, Jacob and Charlotte (pulling no punches). At OUP I want to thank Kathy (for the fork in the road) as well as the fabulous Helen and Debbie whose enthusiasm, creativity and pragmatism have been phenomenal. I'd also like to thank Liz for wielding her own stick to keep the warriors on their path.

In the wider world of martial arts I would like to thank Tom Callos, Sam Yang and Dave Kovar for their clarity and integrity which have constantly translated philosophy into reality. Our Fairfight karate girls in India show us every day that the worst beginnings can still be overcome with kindness and effort. And finally apologies to Professor Stephen Chan (of SOAS Jindokai) whose real life exploits are far more exciting than those of his fictional counterpart.

M.C. STEVENS

PERSEVERANCE – Warriors never lose, because they never quit. You might win, or you might learn but you never give up. A black belt is just a white belt who kept training even when it was tough.

DISCIPLINE – Doing the right thing, even when you don't want to, because it will be worth it. Warriors always try their hardest to do their best.

INDOMITABLE SPIRIT – The fire of the warrior. The crisis may be huge; the danger may be real, but the warrior will dig deep to respond to the threat. In the heat of the battle will be found the true heart of the warrior.